TOP SECRET

TOP SECRET

powered by:

1.

2.

3. →

4.

7.

a

b

c

$x\sqrt{\overline{\begin{array}{|c|c|c|}\hline 3 & \times & 2 \\\hline\end{array}}}$
18

$\begin{array}{r} 3 \cdot 950 \\ \times\ 8 \cdot 19. \\ \hline \end{array}$

CARDBOARD

draw · cut out · stick

2+2+2+2=8

$y\sqrt{8+100\ 87219}$

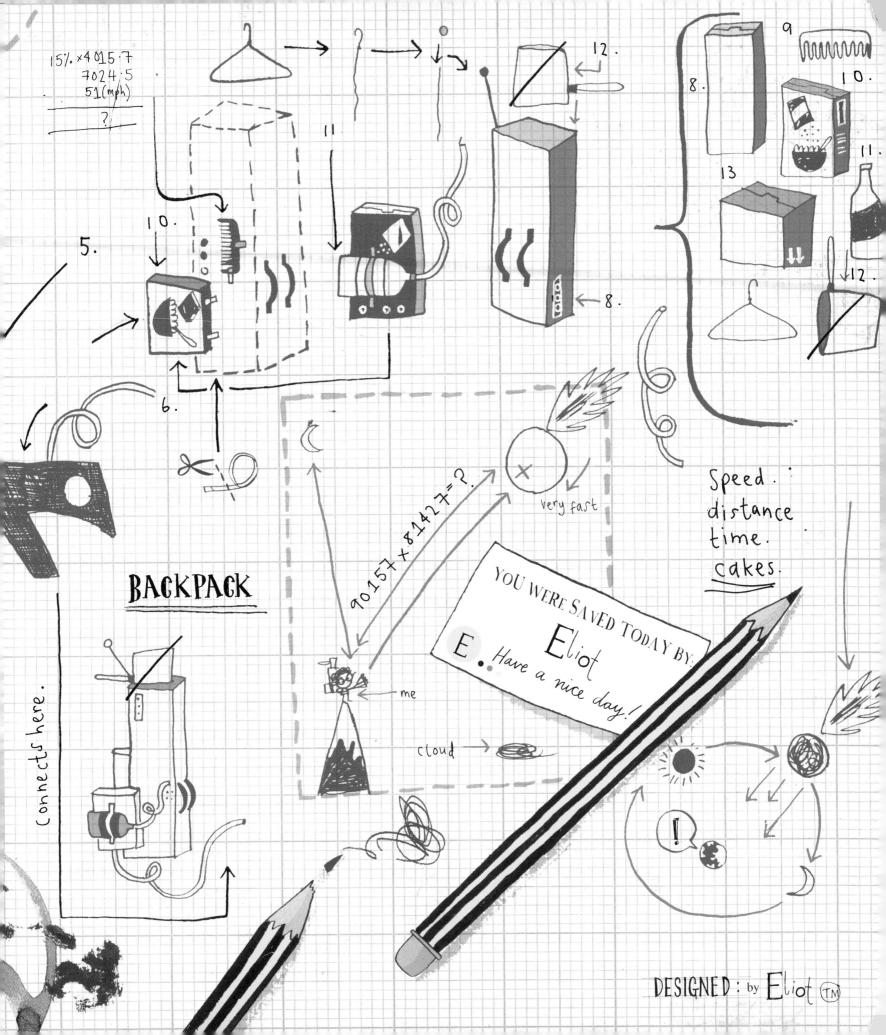

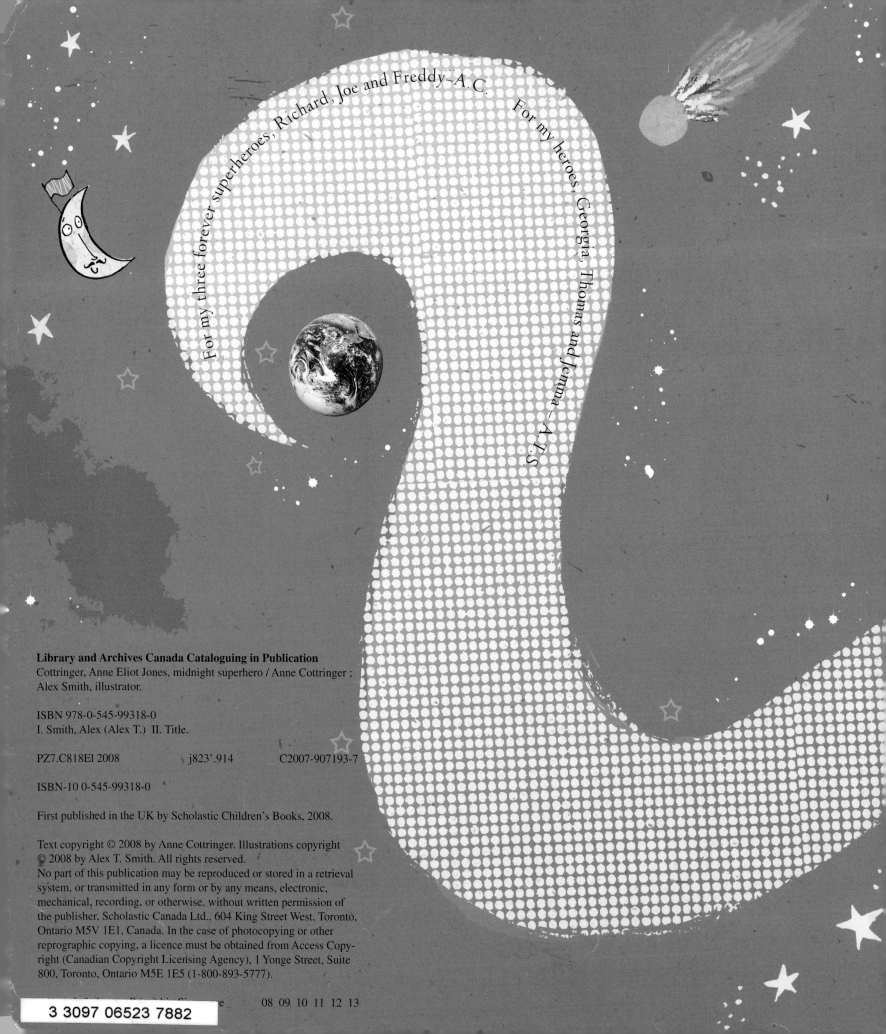

For my three forever superheroes, Richard, Joe and Freddy~A.C.

For my heroes, Georgia, Thomas and Jemma ~ A.T.S.

Library and Archives Canada Cataloguing in Publication
Cottringer, Anne Eliot Jones, midnight superhero / Anne Cottringer ;
Alex Smith, illustrator.

ISBN 978-0-545-99318-0
I. Smith, Alex (Alex T.) II. Title.

PZ7.C818El 2008   j823'.914   C2007-907193-7

ISBN-10 0-545-99318-0

First published in the UK by Scholastic Children's Books, 2008.

08 09 10 11 12 13

ELIOT JONES, MIDNIGHT SUPERHERO

Scholastic Canada Ltd.
Toronto New York London Auckland Sydney
Mexico City New Delhi Hong Kong Buenos Aires

By day,
Eliot is quiet.
He reads his books.
He feeds his goldfish.
He watches Mr. Smith
wash his car.

TIBET

TOY BOX

"Eliot is such a quiet little thing," say all the grownups.

Tick! Tock! Tick! Tock! Tick! Tock!

BONG!

But when the clock strikes *midnight*...

Eliot is a superhero!

He hangs out of helicopters.

He skis down glaciers.

He returns teddies to babies.

Eliot

Sometimes the mayor needs Eliot's help.
"The lions have escaped from the zoo!" he cries. "They're rampaging through the streets!"

Luckily, Eliot is an expert lion tamer.

He leaps from his bedroom window, races through the screaming crowds...

Sometimes the
Coast Guard calls
on his services.

"Help!" they shout.
"A ship is about to CRASH
onto the rocks!"

Luckily, Eliot is a
champion swimmer.

THE RUBBER DUCKY

He dives into the towering waves,
grabs the anchor and tows the ship to safety,
as the sailors shout "Hurray!"

Sometimes the Queen
   requires his assistance.
"A criminal mastermind
   has **stolen** the royal jewels!"
announces the Royal Butler.

Luckily, Eliot is
   an excellent sleuth.

He sneaks into the criminal mastermind's secret hideout.

Tip-toe!

He follows the clues,
cracks the code,
opens the safe...

...and return the jewels
to the grateful Queen.

Tonight, Eliot receives an urgent message from the world's Most Important Scientists.

"A gigantic METEOR is heading this way! It's going to SMASH into the Earth!"

This is Eliot's most important mission ever!

Luckily, Eliot has built a Meteor-Busting Rocket Launcher for just such occasions.

RUSSIA

Unluckily, it's hidden in a deep cave in the mountains of **TIBET** .

The only way to get there before the meteor strikes is by supersonic jet.
Luckily, Eliot is a skilled jet pilot.

Eliot sets off.
Over the Alps.
Over the Caspian Sea.
Across to the Himalayas.

TREASURE!

INDIAN OCEAN

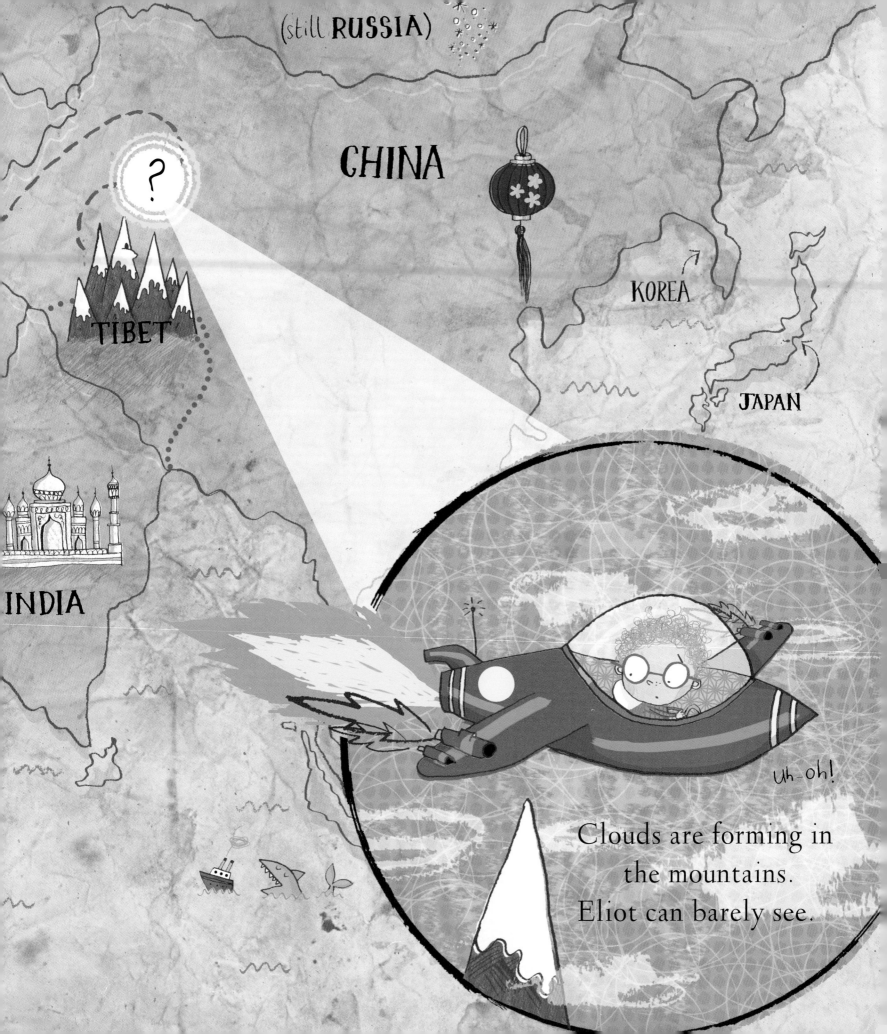

(still **RUSSIA**)

CHINA

KOREA

JAPAN

?

TIBET

INDIA

Uh-oh!

Clouds are forming in
the mountains.
Eliot can barely see.

Suddenly a snow-capped peak
flashes past his window.
Another looms up straight ahead.
Eliot dips his left wing
and swerves just in time.

To reach the cave he must now
land on the shortest,
most dangerous
runway in the world.

He grips
  the controls.
The wheels
  bump the ground.

Screeech!
Eliot skids to a halt.

The sky is blazing with
the light of the meteor.

Closer
and
closer
it comes.

Eliot can see the entrance
to the cave, far above him.
Luckily, Eliot is a highly
experienced mountaineer.
He scrambles up the cliff face,
and into the cave.

Eliot swings the barrel of the
Meteor-Busting Rocket
Launcher towards the sky.

He aims.
He holds his breath.
He waits until just
the right moment...

He fires!

KAPOW!

Eliot **saves** the world from destruction!

The Queen gives Eliot an award for his courage and ingenuity.

The Earth trembles with deafening applause.

But being a
    Midnight Superhero
is very tiring.

It doesn't leave Eliot
    with much energy.
So by day...

Eliot is quiet.

shh!

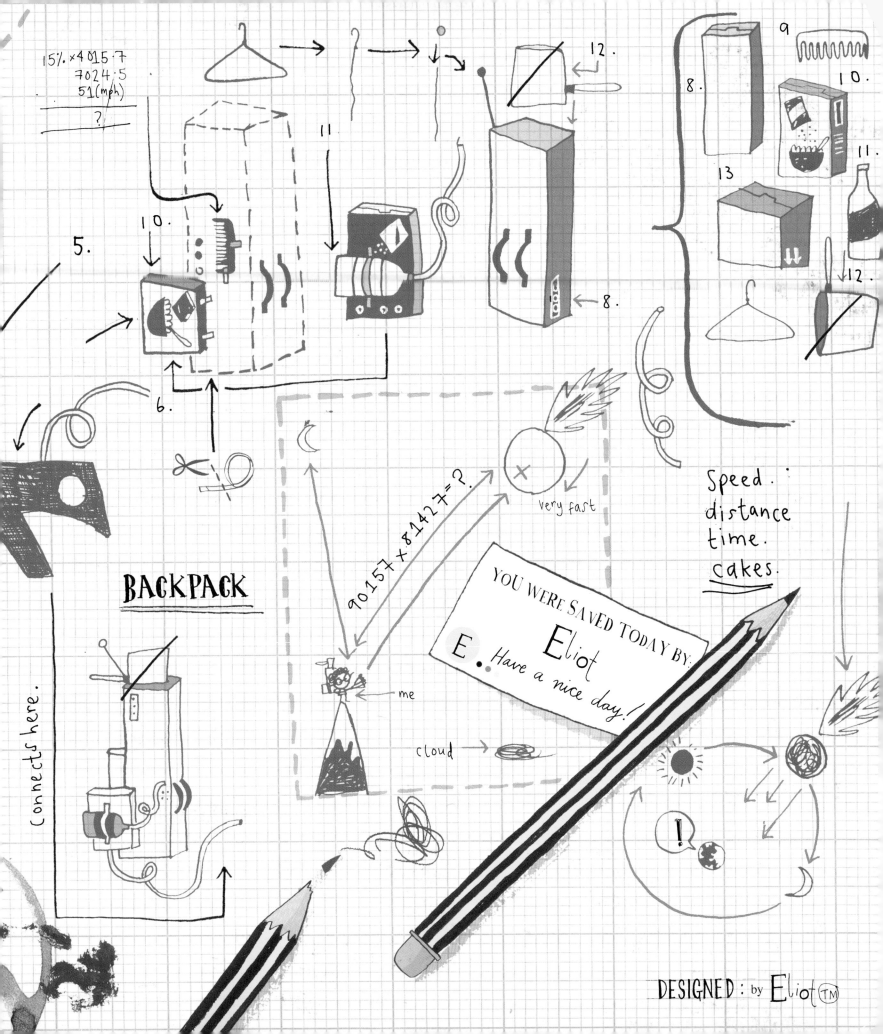